Harry Potter™

DELUXE COLORING BOOK

SCHOLASTIC INC.

New York   Toronto   London   Auckland   Sydney
Mexico City   New Delhi   Hong Kong   Buenos Aires

ISBN-13: 978-0-439-02488-4
ISBN-10: 0-439-02488-9

12 11 10 9 8 7 6 5 4 3 2 1   7 8 9 10 11/0

Book design by Rick DeMonico
Illustrations by Dan Davis, Ted Enik, Josep Miralles, Aristedes Ruiz and various.

Printed in the U.S.A.   First printing, June 2007

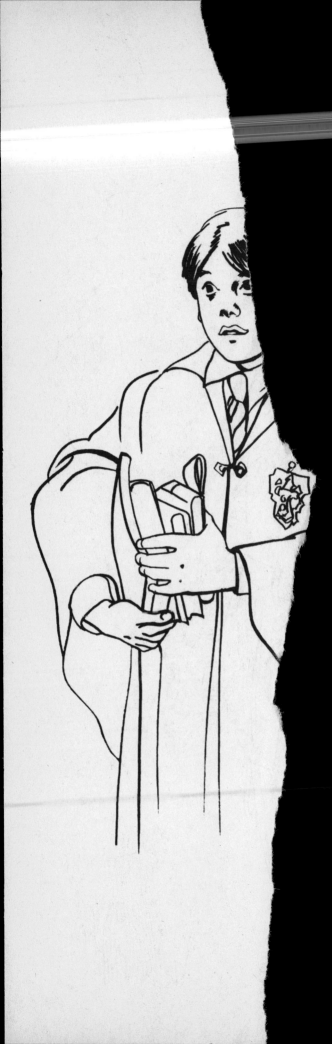

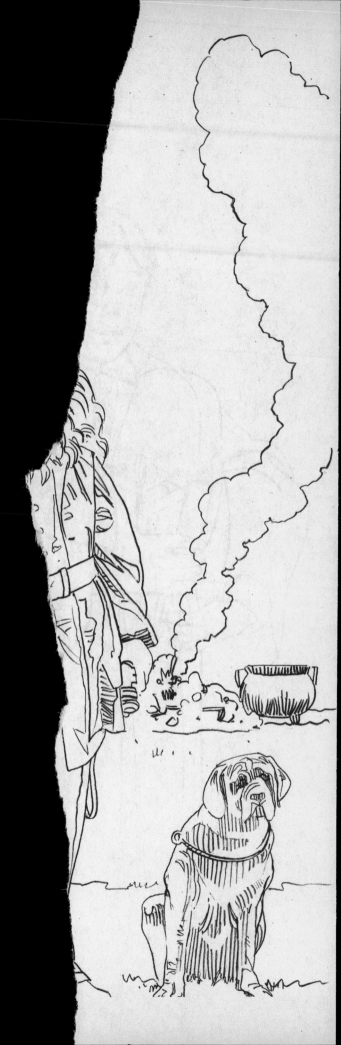

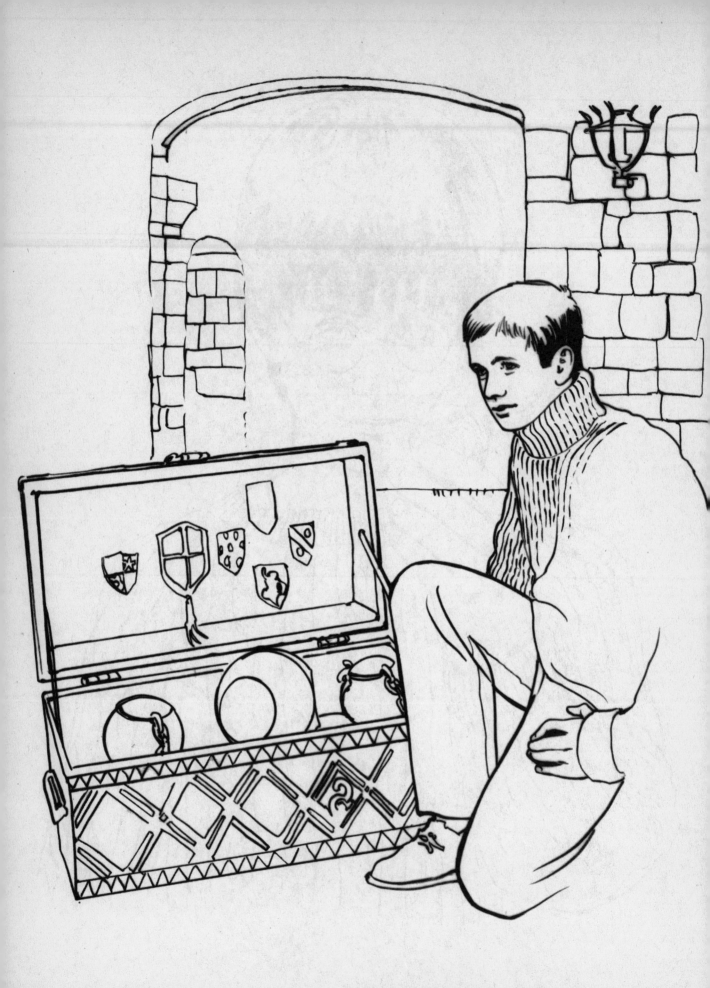

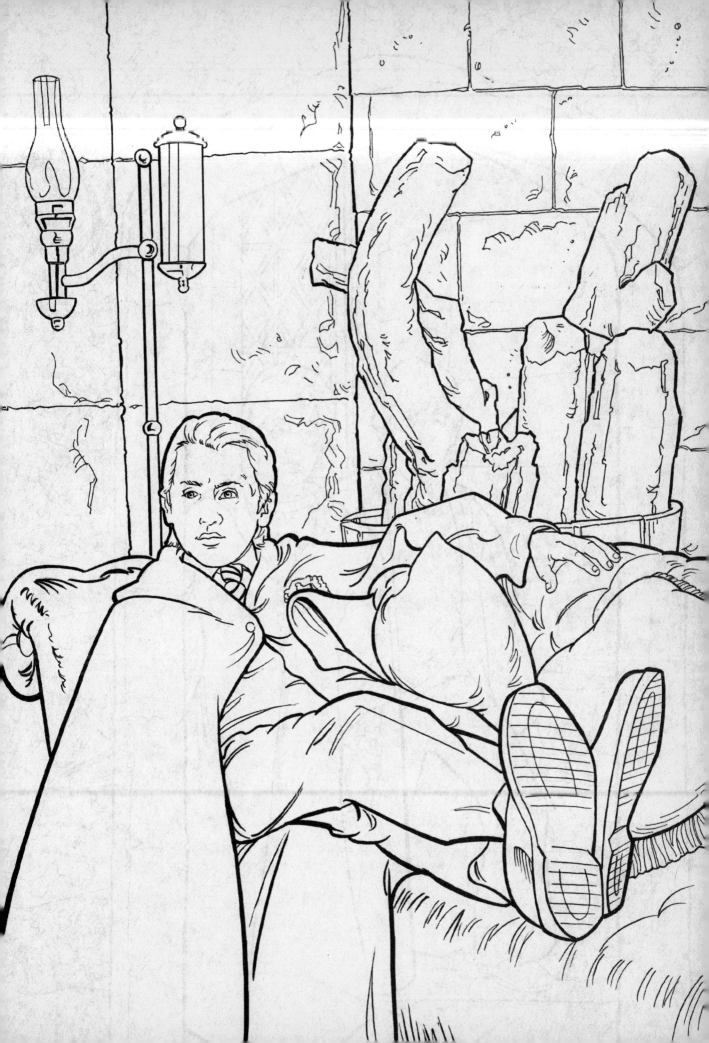

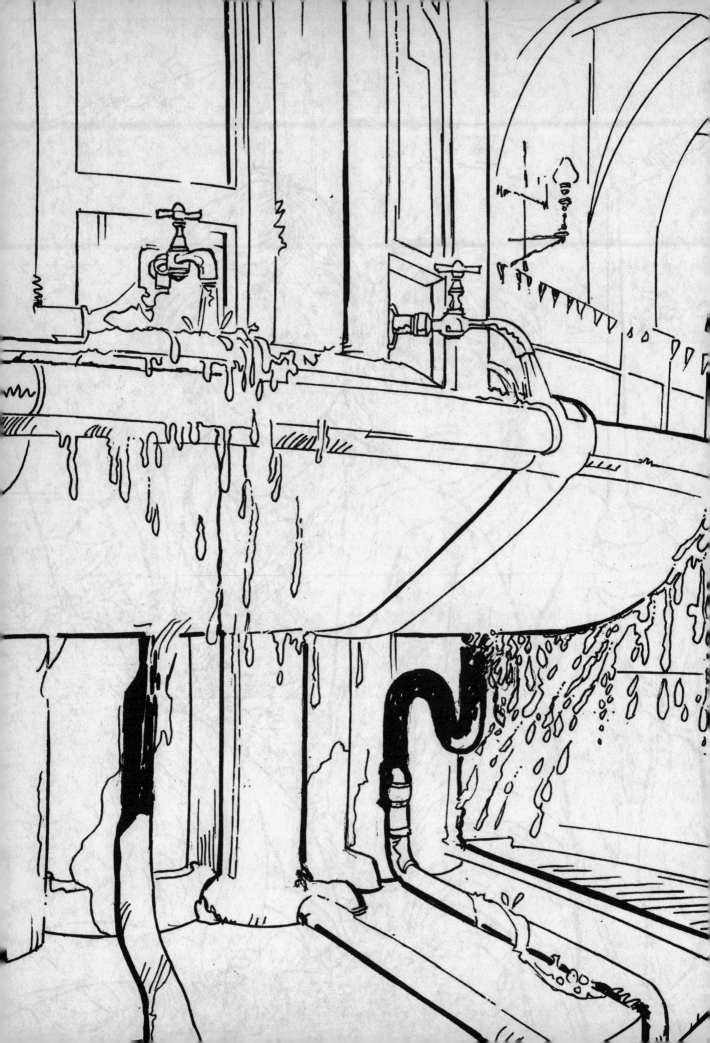

Harry Potter

AND THE
PRISONER
OF AZKABAN™

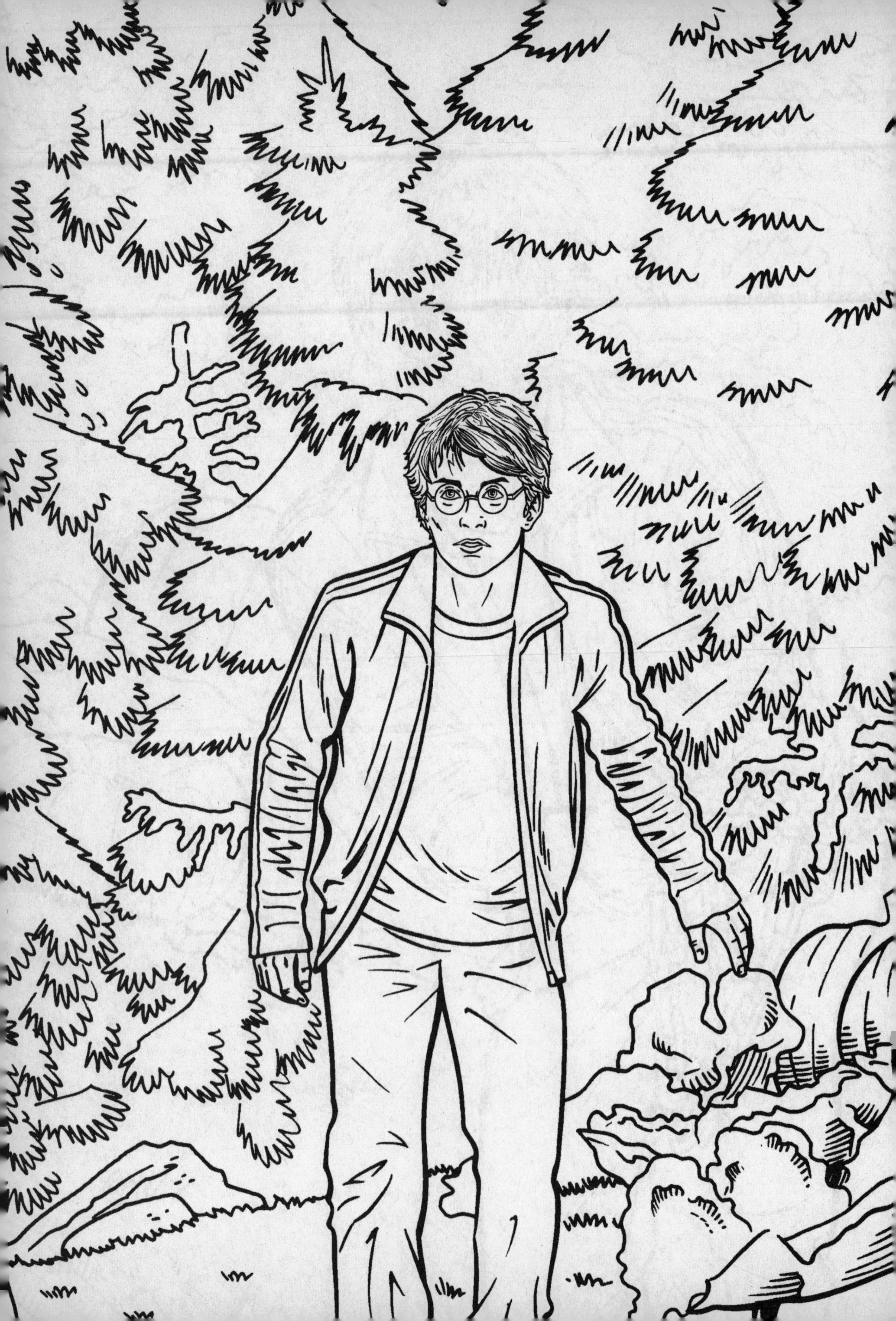

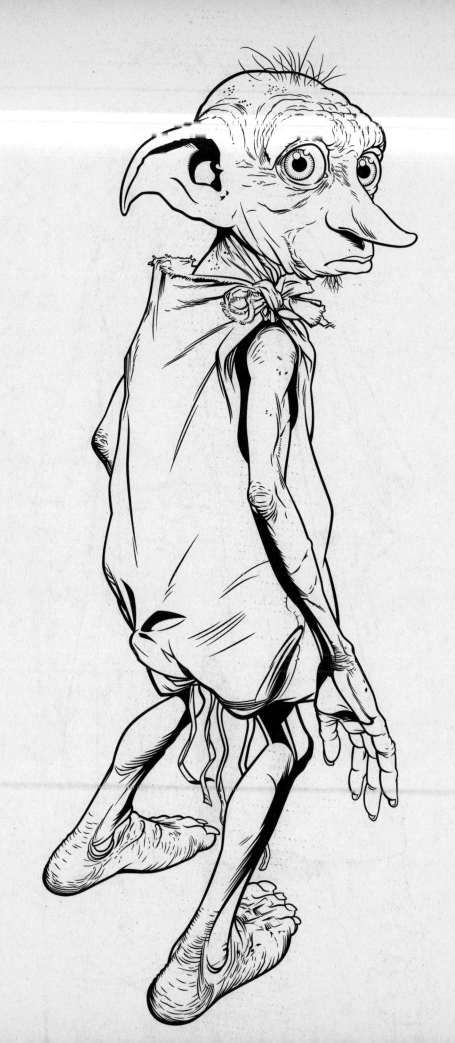

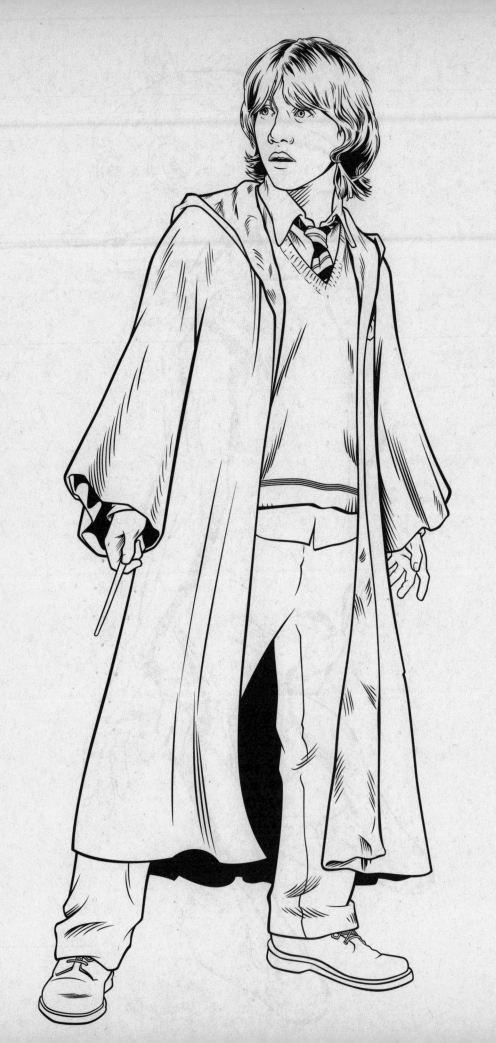

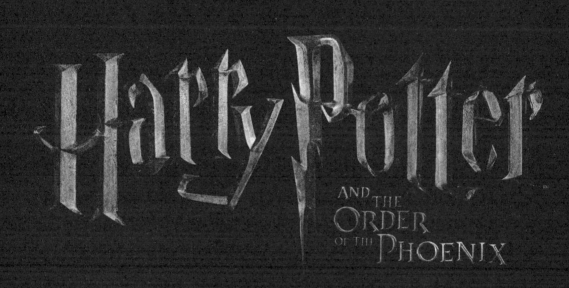